In a creepy old castle
all covered with spines,

lived twelve ugly monsters in two crooked lines.

FRANKENSTEIN

story & pictures by

Ludworst Bemonster

SQUARE
FISH

FEIWEL AND ~~FRIENDS~~ FIENDS · NEW YORK

DEADICATIONS

To the monstrously talented Rock Canyon writers
and illustrators, who never lose their heads
—R.W.

To Hank and George, little monsters
—N.H.

SQUARE
FISH

An Imprint of Macmillan
120 Broadway
New York, NY 10271
mackids.com

Square Fish and the Square Fish logo are trademarks of Macmillan and
are used by Feiwel and Friends under license from Macmillan.

Our books may be purchased in bulk for promotional, educational, or business use. Please
contact your local bookseller or the Macmillan Corporate and Premium Sales Department at
(800) 221-7945 ext. 5442 or by e-mail at MacmillanSpecialMarkets@macmillan.com.

Library of Congress Cataloging-in-Publication Data
Walton, Rick.
Frankenstein / by Ludworst Bemonster; [text by Rick Walton];
[illustrations by Nathan Hale].
p. cm.
Summary: Frankenstein is the scariest of all the monsters in Miss Devel's castle until one night when he loses his head.
ISBN 978-1-250-07946-6 (paperback)
[1. Stories in rhyme. 2. Monsters—Fiction.] I. Hale, Nathan, ill. II. Title.
PZ8.3.W199Fr 2012   [E]—dc23   2011014804

Originally published in the United States by Feiwel and Friends
First Square Fish Edition: 2016
Square Fish logo designed by Filomena Tuosto

The artwork was created with Kuretake brush pens and Rapidograph Ultradraw ink.
It was colored with M. Graham Watercolors and Photoshop.

5 7 9 10 8 6
AR: 0.5 / LEXILE: 430L

In two crooked lines, they bonked their heads,

pulled out their teeth,

and wet their beds.

They bit the good

and gobbled the bad.

They even tried to devour your dad!

They left the castle
each night at nine
in crooked lines.

They yelled.

They whined.

The ugliest one was Frankenstein.

He scared people out of their socks.

He could even frighten rocks.

When he visited the zoo,
animals hid and cried, "Boo-hoo!"

And nobody knew so well
how to torment Miss Devel.

One bleak and dark and dismal night,
Miss Devel turned on her light
and whispered, "Something is not right."

Instead of shrieks and howls and groans,
Frankenstein laid still—no moans.

Devel screeched, "Call Doctor Bone!"

who came, then screamed, and grabbed his phone . . .

and dialed, FrankenSTEIN-ONE-ONE.

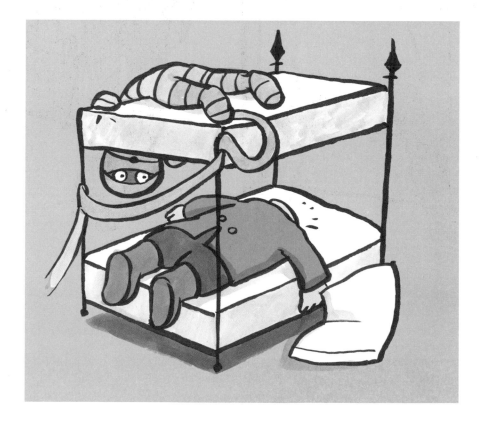

"Nurse," he said, "his noggin's gone!"

All the other monsters said,
"It wasn't *me* who ate his head!"

Frankenstein was carried off in
Doctor Bone's creaky coffin.

In a hearse grotesque and gory,
they drove him to the laboratory.

When Frankenstein awoke, he said,

"What's this? I have a brand-new head!"

His head was hungry, so he swallowed
the nursing staff; the doctor followed.

He chomped the ceiling out of habit.

Yum! he thought. *It tastes like rabbit!*

He even ate a pizza guy,

and so, ten days passed quickly by.

One stormy eve, Miss Devel said,

"Isn't it a fine—

night to bother

Frankenstein?"

VISITORS FROM TWO TO FOUR

read a sign nailed to his door.

The monsters gnawed the wood and then
shouted out, "We're coming in!"

In they stomped, then squealed, "SWEET!"
For there around them, at their feet
were lots of yucky treats to eat.

But what inspired the greatest *"Eeeews"*?

There on his neck:

two huge new screws!

"Miss Devel, we want to stay."

But Miss Devel replied, "No way!"

Home they trudged, and bonked their heads,

pulled out their teeth,

and wet their beds.

One bleak and dark and dismal night,
Miss Devel turned on her light
and shouted, "Something is not right!"

And hoping for no more disaster,

Miss Devel ran fast

and faster.

"Oh," she pleaded. "Monsters, do
tell me what is troubling you."

All the ugly monsters said—

nothing. Each had lost his head!

"Good night, monsters!
Now, you *cannot* whine and yell!
I'm going back to sleep!"
said Miss Devel.

And she turned out the light—

And slammed the door—

And that's all there is—

There isn't any more.